Little Sister

Karen's Goldfish

Ann M. Martin

Illustrations by Susan Tang

A
LITTLE APPLE
PAPERBACK

SCHOLASTIC INC.
New York Toronto London Auckland Sydney

ISBN 0-590-43644-9

12 11 10 9 8 7 6 5 4 3   1 2 3 4 5 6/9

Printed in the U.S.A.   40

First Scholastic printing, March 1991

For Sara and Matt
from Aunt Martin

Karen's Goldfish

Good-bye, Emily Junior

"Emily!" I called. "Emily, where are you?"

I looked all around my room. I could not see Emily Junior anywhere.

"Emily!" I called again, even though Emily does not know her name. She does not come when I call.

Emily Junior is a rat. A real one, I mean. She is white, except for her eyes, her tail, and her nose. They are pink.

I checked under my bed again. I looked in every one of my shoes in the closet.

"EMILY!" I shouted. "YOU COME OUT

1

HERE RIGHT THIS INSTANT. . . . Okay, I'm going to count to ten. I have to go to Daddy's house soon, and if I can't find you, Mommy will be very unhappy. One, two, three, four — "

Emily poked her nose out from under my bureau.

"There you are!" I scooped up Emily and held her tight. "Oh, I hate saying good-bye to you," I told her. "I hate leaving you behind when Andrew and I go to Daddy's. But that's the way things are."

I bet if Emily could talk, she would have said, "I will miss you, too, Karen."

I am Karen Brewer. I am seven years old. I have blonde hair, blue eyes, freckles, and a little brother. My brother's name is Andrew and he is four, going on five. He is shy. (I am not.)

Most of the time, Andrew and I live at our mommy's house. But every other weekend we live at Daddy's. When we go to Daddy's, I have to leave Emily behind. I do not like that at all.

I tried to say good-bye to Emily, but I could not. Then I got an idea. Maybe I could sneak Emily over to Daddy's house! I pulled my shirt away from my neck. I started to drop Emily down my shirt, but I heard Andrew running up the stairs. Quickly, I pulled Emily out.

"What are your doing?" asked Andrew.

"Just saying good-bye to Emily Junior," I told him. I stuck Emily in her cage. "I hate leaving Emily here."

"Yeah," said Andrew, even though Emily is my pet, not his.

"At Daddy's house are Shannon and Boo-Boo" (they are a puppy and an old, mean cat), "but they aren't really ours," I said.

"No," agreed Andrew with a sigh. "Shannon is David Michael's and Boo-Boo is Daddy's." Andrew sighed again. Then he said, "I wish we had a pet of our own at the big house."

"Me, too!" I exclaimed.

"I would like a puppy just like David Michael's."

"And I would like a cat, but not like Boo-Boo. Boo-Boo is too old. He scratches and spits. I would like a sweet little kitten."

"No, a puppy," said Andrew.

"Oh, it doesn't matter," I said. "A cat or a dog. What's the difference? As long as you and I could have a pet at Daddy's house."

"Well, we can't," said Andrew.

"How do you know?" I asked.

Andrew shrugged.

"You know what?" (I had suddenly gotten another idea.) "Maybe we *could* have a pet at Daddy's. We've never asked. But if I tell Daddy how much we would like a pet at the big house, maybe he will say yes. I will talk to Daddy this weekend. Okay, Andrew?"

"Okay."

"Karen! Andrew!" Mommy called then. "Time to go to Daddy's."

Two Mommies,
Two Daddies

Andrew and I live at two different houses — Mommy's house and Daddy's house. This is because our mommy and daddy are divorced. A long time ago, they used to be married. They loved each other very much. So they had Andrew and me. Then they stopped loving each other. They still loved Andrew and me, but they did not love each other anymore. That was when they got divorced. Daddy stayed in the big house. He had grown up there. The house was built by Great-great-grandfather Brewer. It is a Brewer house. Mommy moved to a smaller house. She brought Andrew and me with her. The little house is not too far away from the big house. Both houses are in Stoneybrook, Connecticut. That is a good thing since Andrew and I live at the little house *and* the big house.

Do you know what? After Mommy and Daddy had been divorced for awhile, they each got married again. Mommy married Seth. Seth moved into the little house with us. He brought along his dog, Midgie, and his cat, Rocky. I like Seth because he likes animals and children. Seth is my stepfather. (I guess that makes Midgie my stepdog and Rocky my stepcat.)

Daddy married a woman named Elizabeth. Elizabeth is my stepmother. She is very nice. Thank goodness Daddy's house is a mansion, because an awful lot of people live in it. Besides Daddy and Elizabeth, there are Elizabeth's four kids. They are

Charlie, who is seventeen, and Sam, who is fifteen (they go to high school), David Michael, who is seven like me, and Kristy. Kristy is thirteen. I just love Kristy. She is the nicest person I know. I am glad she is my big stepsister.

You know who else lives at the big house? Emily Michelle. She is two and a half. She is my adopted sister. Daddy and Elizabeth adopted her from a faraway country called Vietnam. Emily does not talk much yet, but I like her anyway. That is why I named my rat after her.

There is still *another* person living at the big house. She is Nannie. Nannie is Elizabeth's mother. That makes her my stepgrandmother. Nannie moved in when Emily came to stay. Nannie takes care of Emily while Daddy and Elizabeth are at work. She is another one of my favorite people. She bowls and cooks and has lots of friends. She does not seem old at all.

Since Andrew and I have two of so many things, I call us Andrew Two-Two and

Karen Two-Two. (I got the names from a book my teacher read to our class. It was called *Jacob Two-Two Meets the Hooded Fang*.) Anyway, Andrew and I have two mommies and two daddies, two families, two houses, two cats and two dogs (well, they are not *really* ours), and two of lots of other things. I have two stuffed cats (Moosie at the big house, Goosie at the little house). We have clothes and toys and books at each house. That is helpful, because then we don't have to pack much when we go back and forth between Mommy's and Daddy's. I even have two best friends. Nancy Dawes lives next door to the little house. Hannie Papadakis lives across the street and one house down from the big house. Nancy and Hannie and I are all in Ms. Colman's second-grade class at Stoneybrook Academy.

You know what *else* I have two of? I have two pairs of glasses, pink and blue. One pair is for reading; the other pair is for the rest of the time.

Mostly, being a two-two is fun. I like

my big-house family and my little-house family — for different reasons. But sometimes I wish I were a one-one again. And that Mommy and Daddy were still married.

What Pet to Get

At the big house that night, we had a happy, noisy supper. (I like the noise and the bustle at the big house; Andrew does not.) Everyone was there — Daddy, Elizabeth, Kristy, Charlie, Sam, David Michael, Emily, Nannie, Andrew, me, and even Shannon and Boo-Boo. (Of course, Shannon and Boo-Boo were not sitting at the table. They were just hanging around the kitchen.)

As soon as dinner was over, Andrew whispered to me, "When are you going to talk to Daddy and Elizabeth?"

"Shh. In a little while. When things calm down."

"Okay," said Andrew.

I waited until the kitchen had been cleaned up. I waited until Charlie had gone off with some of his friends. I waited until Emily had been put to bed. I waited until Kristy had left to go baby-sitting. (Kristy loves to baby-sit. She even formed a club with some of her friends. The club is a sitting business. Kristy is the president.) Then I waited until Daddy and Elizabeth were reading the paper in the living room.

The house was much quieter.

"Come on, Andrew," I said. "Let's go talk to Daddy."

"Me, too? I thought *you* were going to talk to him."

"I am. But I think it might be good for you to come, too. I can remind Daddy and Elizabeth that you don't have a pet of your own at *either* house. At least I have Emily Junior at Mommy's. But you have no pet at all. So come with me, and look very, very sad while I tell Daddy how much we would like a big-house pet."

"A dog," said Andrew.

"A cat," I said. "Oh, well. Who cares? Now is the time to talk."

I took Andrew by the hand. We walked into the living room.

I cleared my throat. "Excuse us," I said.

Daddy and Elizabeth put their papers down. "Yes?" said Daddy.

"Andrew and I have something to ask you," I replied. "I know you probably won't let us do this." (I have found that when you really, really want something, if you say you don't expect to get it, then parents are more likely to give it to you after all.)

"What do you want to do?" asked Daddy.

"Get a pet," I told him. "A pet for Andrew and me at the big house. Daddy, you have Boo-Boo, and David Michael has Shannon. And at Mommy's are Rocky and Midgie, but they belong to Seth. I have Emily Junior, of course, but she has to stay at the little house. And poor, poor Andrew doesn't have any pet of his own."

I glanced at Andrew. He looked like he was going to burst into tears.

Then Daddy and Elizabeth glanced at each other. Daddy said, "Why don't you two go into the den? Elizabeth and I would like to talk in private."

"Okay," I replied. And we did go into the den. I thought about standing around in the hall so I could eavesdrop. But I decided I better not.

Andrew and I waited and waited.

At last Daddy and Elizabeth came into the den. Daddy announced, "We have made a decision."

"Yes?" I said.

"You may get a pet."

"All *right!*" I cried.

And Andrew grinned.

Goldfishies

"**A** pet! A big-house pet of our own!" I shouted. "Isn't that great, Andrew? Isn't that the best?"

"Yup," said Andrew. Then he added, "Thank you, Daddy. Thank you, Elizabeth."

So I said the same thing.

"You're welcome," they replied.

"But," Daddy went on, "before you get a pet, you have to make two promises."

"All right," I replied slowly.

"The first," said Daddy, "is that the pet must be very small and very easy to care for. In other words, no more cats or dogs. This house is wild enough already."

"What about a monkey?" asked Andrew. "Could we get a monkey?"

"No," Daddy answered. "Much too wild."

"Your father," Elizabeth said, "means that you must promise to get a small pet that will stay in a cage. A mouse, a hamster, or a guinea pig. Something like that."

"We promise," I told her. "What's our second promise?"

"Your second promise," replied Daddy, "is that you find somebody here to take care of the pet while you're at Mommy's house. And don't ask Nannie. She's got her hands full."

"Don't ask Emily Michelle, either," said Elizabeth, and I giggled.

After Andrew and I made our second promise, we tore upstairs to the playroom. We had to decide what kind of pet to get.

"A snake," said Andrew as soon as we were sitting on the floor.

"No way," I replied.

"How about a frog or a turtle?"

"No. No gross green things. Let's get a guinea pig. Or a gerbil."

"But you already have a rat at Mommy's. That's sort of the same."

"Well, we're *not* getting a snake."

"But I *want* one!" cried Andrew.

"But getting a big-house pet was my idea," I pointed out. "So — Hey, I know! How about a fish? They're *really* small."

"A goldfishie?" said Andrew.

"Whatever. A fish is perfect. Maybe Daddy would even let us get two."

"Yeah!" exclaimed Andrew.

"Now we just have to find someone to take care of the fish when we're not here."

"What about Charlie?" suggested Andrew.

I shook my head. "Charlie and Sam and even Kristy might think fish are for babies. Besides, they're too busy. David Michael would probably do it, though."

So we asked David Michael if he would feed our fish, if we got one.

"I don't know," David Michael replied. "I already have to take care of Shannon."

"The fish could be part yours," I told him. "He would really be Andrew's and mine, but he could be part yours — when we're not around."

"Okay," agreed David Michael. "I like fish."

"Terrific! Thank you!" I said.

Then Andrew and I ran back down to the living room.

"We've decided what we want," I announced to Daddy and Elizabeth. "A goldfish. It will be very small. And David Michael said he would take care of it."

"A fish sounds fine," said Daddy.

I paused. Then I asked, "How about two fish — one for Andrew and one for me? They wouldn't be too much trouble. Besides, one fish would get lonely all by itself."

"Two fish it is, then," said Daddy.

We were all set. The very next day, Daddy and Elizabeth would take Andrew and me to the pet store!

Too Many Fish

On Saturday morning, I was gigundo excited. So was Andrew. We could not *wait* to go to the pet store. But we had to wait for awhile. We had to wait until breakfast was over. We had to wait until the kitchen was cleaned up. We had to wait to make sure that someone would be at home to watch David Michael and Emily. At last, Daddy and Elizabeth were ready to go.

The four of us climbed into the station wagon, and Elizabeth drove us downtown.

She parked in front of the pet store. Andrew and I flew out of the car as soon as it had stopped.

"Come on, Andrew!" I cried. "Let's look at the fish!"

In the pet store, we found a whole *wall* of them. Aquarium after aquarium of brightly colored fish. Some were big, some were tiny; some were pretty, some were not so pretty; some looked fierce, some looked gentle.

"Andrew," I began. "How are we ever going to choose our pets? There are too many fish here."

"Why don't you walk from one end of the wall to the other," suggested Daddy. "That way, you can see everything."

"Okay. That's a good idea," I replied.

So Andrew and I examined the fish in every tank. A saleswoman helped us. She told us which fish would not get along, and which fish were hard to care for. And Daddy told us which fish were too expensive.

Finally, Andrew and I were standing in front of one aquarium.

"A goldfishie," said Andrew. "That's what I want."

"I think I'll get one, too." I looked at Daddy and Elizabeth. "Two goldfish? Is that okay?" I asked.

"Fine," replied Elizabeth.

Then came the hardest part of all — choosing the right fish. Andrew and I stared and stared at the tank. After about five minutes, Andrew said, "I want that one." He pointed to a large fish. Its color was brighter than most of the others, and it was perfectly shaped.

While the saleswoman was scooping up the fish in a net, I kept on looking. At last I noticed a small fish that was not perfectly shaped. And on its tail was a black spot. It was different from the other fish.

I fell in love with it.

"I'll take it," I told the saleswoman.

So my fish was scooped out of the tank,

too. The woman put both fish into a cardboard box full of water. Then she said, "Do you have an aquarium at home?"

"No," said Daddy. "We thought we'd just put the fish into a bowl."

"An aquarium is really better. It's healthier for the fish."

"Okay," said Daddy.

"And you'll need a filter, a light, an air pump, a thermometer, plants, gravel, and, of course, fish food."

Daddy didn't look too happy about this, but he bought everything anyway. Plus a book on how to care for fish, and a very beautiful little castle to set at the bottom of the tank. The fish could swim through the windows and doors. It was sort of a goldfish playground.

We had bought an awful lot of stuff. When we left the store, Daddy was carrying the aquarium. Elizabeth was carrying the other things. And Andrew and I were both holding the container with our fish in it.

"I cannot wait to get home!" I said. "Thank you, Daddy."

"You're welcome," he replied. "But you and Andrew and David Michael have a big responsibility now."

Goldfishie and Crystal Light

As soon as we got home, Daddy and Andrew and I went to the playroom. We put the aquarium on a table. Then Daddy began fiddling with things. He set up the filter, the light, the air pump, and the thermometer.

"Let me pour the gravel into the tank!" Andrew cried.

"I want to put the castle in," I said.

When the tank was filled with water, it was time to put our fish into it. Since Andrew and I each wanted to do that, I opened one flap of the box and Andrew opened the other. Then we both held onto the box. Together we dumped it over the tank. The goldfish fell into the water. They began swimming around. Andrew and I could not take our eyes off them.

Daddy said, "The fish are your responsibility now. Aren't there a couple of things you need to do?"

"Feed them," said Andrew.

"Put the lid on the tank so Boo-Boo won't get them," I said. "Also, I better read the book about caring for fish."

"Good," said Daddy. "I'll leave you alone now."

Andrew fed the fish. He put the lid on the tank.

I settled down with the book. After I'd been reading for awhile, I said to my brother, "You know? Fish aren't as easy to take care of as I thought they would be. We will have to check the thermometer all the time to make sure the water isn't too hot or too cold for the fish. We will have to make sure the water doesn't have any bad chemicals in it. We have to keep the plants alive, we have to be sure the pump and the filter are working, and we can*not* overfeed the fish. Boy, I sure hope David Michael can handle this. I hope he understands everything. I am going to make him read the fish book." And, I thought, the only thing Andrew will be able to do is feed the fish. The other things are too hard for him.

Late that afternoon, Andrew and I stood in front of the aquarium. With the light on, the fish looked even more brilliant than they had in the store.

"We better name our fish," I said to Andrew. "Every pet needs a name."

Andrew nodded. "Mine is named Goldfishie."

I thought and thought and thought. Should I give my fish a person's name? A funny name? No. My fish needed a beautiful name. So I decided it was a girl. I called her Crystal Light.

*　　*　　*

On Sunday, about half an hour before Mommy and Seth would come to pick up Andrew and me, I had a talk with David Michael.

"Taking care of fish is hard work," I told him.

David Michael nodded seriously.

"You have to keep the equipment going, and you have to make sure the water temperature is always right."

"Okay."

"Now here's the fish book. Make sure you read the whole thing," I said bossily.

"Yes, teacher," replied David Michael, smiling. Then he went on, "You *know* I'm going to take good care of Goldfishie and Crystal Light. I'm older than you are, and — "

"Only a few months older."

From outside came the sound of Mommy's car honking.

"Karen!" shouted Andrew. "Mommy and Seth are here! Come downstairs."

"Don't you want to say good-bye to Gold-fishie first? I want to say good-bye to Crystal Light."

So Andrew and I kissed the side of the aquarium. "Good-bye!" we said. We would not see our new pets for two weeks.

Crystal Light,
My Delight

One afternoon, I was supposed to be doing homework. But I could not. I was daydreaming. I was thinking about my fish.

"Crystal Light, my delight. Crystal Light, my delight," I sang over and over.

And then I got up to do what I'd done several times since I'd come back to the little house. I went into Mommy's room. I dialed the phone.

"Hello?" said Charlie on the other end of the line.

"Hello. It's me, Karen."

"You're not calling about the fish again, are you?"

"Well, yes," I admitted.

"Karen, they're just fine. They were fine when you called this morning. They were fine when you called both times yesterday. They were fine when you called both times the day before that. David Michael is taking very good care of Goldfishie and Crystal Light."

I sighed. "I just wish I could see them myself."

Charlie did not say anything.

So I had to ask, "Charlie? Do you think you could drive me over to Daddy's so I could see Crystal Light? I really miss her."

It was Charlie's turn to sigh. "Oh, Karen . . ."

"Please? Just drive the Junk Bucket over." (That's what we call Charlie's car, which is a used car.) "Then pick me up and take me back to Daddy's. I want to see Crystal Light.

I'll only stay a minute. Well, a few minutes. I just want to make sure that Crystal Light really is okay."

"All right," said Charlie. "Let me talk to your mom first, though."

So Charlie talked to Mommy. And soon I was sitting next to him in his car. When we reached the big house, I thanked Charlie. Then I raced inside, and upstairs to the playroom. For a moment, I just stood in the doorway with my eyes closed. When I opened them . . . there was the aquarium on its table. The light was on. The filter was on. I breathed a sigh of relief.

"Hi, Crystal Light!" I called.

I ran across the room and kissed the side of the aquarium.

Crystal Light was swimming around happily. She was waving her tail in the water. Back and forth, back and forth went the fin with the black spot.

Goldfishie looked fine, too. He was swimming in and out of the castle.

I heard a noise then and realized that David Michael was standing next to me. He was looking at the aquarium, too. Then he looked at me.

I knew what he wanted to say. He wanted to say, "See? I told you I could take good care of your fish."

I did not let him say that. I said it for him.

"You took good care of our fish after all. Thanks."

"You're welcome," replied David Michael. "I like to take care of them. Especially when I can pretend they're mine."

Not much later, Charlie drove me back to the little house in the Junk Bucket. When I got inside, I ran to find Andrew.

"Guess what!" I cried.

"What?" asked Andrew. (He was watching *Sesame Street*.)

"Crystal Light and Goldfishie are fine. I saw them myself. David Michael is taking good care of them. They look very happy."

Andrew smiled. "Good," he said. "When can I see them?"

"The next time we go to the big house," I replied.

"Yea!" cried Andrew.

The Saddest Thing

Finally there were just two days left before Andrew and I would go to the big house. Two more days until we could see Crystal Light and Goldfishie again.

I made up a new song. It did not *exactly* rhyme, but I think that is okay. This was my song: *Two more days, two more nights. Then I'll see . . . my delight!*

On Wednesday, good things happened in school. Ricky Torres (we are sort of married) gave me some candy at lunchtime. During gym I walked from one end of the balance beam to the other — without falling off! And Hannie Papadakis asked if Nancy and I wanted to go to a petting zoo with her family one day soon.

So I was in a good mood when I came home from school on Wednesday. I was in such a good mood that instead of playing at Nancy's that afternoon, I asked Andrew if he wanted to play with me. He was looking lonely.

But when I said I would help him learn a new magic trick, he looked very happy. (Andrew loves magic. He has a box of tricks. But since he cannot read yet, he does not know how to make most of the tricks work. I have to help him with the instructions.)

I was just about to show Andrew how to make a penny disappear, when the phone rang. I leaped up from the floor.

"I'll get it!" I screamed.

"Indoor voice, Karen," Mommy reminded me.

"Okay," I said as I picked up the phone. Guess who was calling. Daddy!

But he said, "Karen, I have some very bad news for you. David Michael just called me here at work. He said that Crystal Light died today."

"Nooo!" I howled. "How did that happen?"

"We're not sure. David Michael was taking good care of the fish. But when he came home from school today, Crystal Light was floating at the top of the tank."

"That is not fair!" I began to cry. "I want to see Crystal Light. David Michael didn't flush her already, did he?"

"No," said Daddy. "He put her in a little box. It's up to you to decide what to do with your fish." I just sniffled and didn't say anything. So Daddy went on, "Let me talk to Mommy, okay?"

"Okay," I said.

Mommy and Daddy talked for a few minutes. Then they got off the phone. Mommy led me into the living room. She hugged me for a long time. When I was not crying so much anymore, she said, "Your father is on his way over here. He will take you to see Crystal Light."

I nodded. But I could not talk.

Soon Daddy rang our doorbell. I walked slowly to the car with him. As we drove along, I stopped crying.

Daddy glanced at me.

"It's not fair!" I said again. "Goldfishie is still alive and Crystal Light is dead. Andrew has a pet at the big house, and I don't."

I began to feel angry. I was angry at David Michael. How could he have let Crystal Light die? Why hadn't he taken better care of my fish? I told him and *told* him about the fish and their tank.

I guess he did not pay enough attention.

I sat silently until Daddy pulled into the driveway of the big house.

"Karen?" he said. Are you all right?"

I nodded slowly. "It's just that when someone or something dies, it's the saddest thing."

Daddy stroked my hair. "Let's go inside," he said.

Fish-Killer!

I got out of the car. I ran ahead of Daddy.
I beat him to the front door of the big house.
I let myself inside. Then I raced upstairs.
I didn't stop running until I was in the
playroom, standing in front of the fish tank.

In the tank was Goldfishie. He swam
around and around.

All by himself.

At least he was alive.

I examined the aquarium and the water.
Everything looked okay. Everything was
hooked up and working.

I could not figure out how David Michael had killed Crystal Light.

After I finished looking at Goldfishie, I looked at the table the tank was sitting on. I saw a small, white box. It was made of cardboard. It was the kind of box jewelry comes in — but now it was Crystal Light's coffin.

I did not want to look inside the box. I knew I had to, though. So I lifted the lid. Crystal Light lay on her side on the little bed of cotton. At first I started to cry again, but then I noticed something. Crystal Light was very still. But she did not look sick or hurt.

"Maybe she's just taking a nap."

I did not even realize I had said that out loud until I heard Daddy say softly, "Karen . . ."

I turned around. Daddy and David Michael were watching me. I did not care. I lifted Crystal Light out of the box. Then I placed her very carefully in the tank.

"Karen," said Daddy again. "Crystal

Light won't swim. She's dead, honey."

"No she isn't." I watched my fish for a long time. She just bobbed on top of the water. Then I knew that Daddy was right.

Crystal Light really was dead.

So I scooped her up and put her back in her coffin. Then I yelled, "David Michael, this is your fault!"

"No, it isn't," he cried.

"Yes, it is. You did something wrong. You didn't take good care of Crystal Light. You know what you are? You are a fish-killer!"

"All right, Karen," said Daddy. "That's enough. Time to go home."

I let Daddy drive me home. But I did not apologize to David Michael.

Back at the little house, Andrew said, "I'm sorry Crystal Light died."

"Thanks."

"Want to play checkers?"

"Checkers? No, I do not want to play checkers. How could you — "

"Karen!" exclaimed Mommy. "Andrew was just trying to be nice."

"Sorry," I mumbled. But Andrew was already crying.

I did not feel *too* sorry for him, though. He still had Goldfishie. Crystal Light was gone forever.

I began to cry, too.

That night, Andrew and I could not eat dinner. Andrew said he wasn't hungry. And I could not stop crying.

All evening, I moped around my room. I did not do my homework. I kept looking at Emily Junior in her cage. "I hope you're not going to die, too," I told her.

"Karen! Andrew! Bedtime!" called Mommy just then.

"Okay," I replied. I lay down on my bed, even though I was still dressed. I fell asleep. Mommy found me later. She took off my shoes and pulled the covers over me.

I never felt a thing.

When I woke up, I thought of Crystal Light right away.

Karen the Sad

I felt happy.

Crystal Light was alive after all! It was hard to believe, but then, so are lots of things. Like how the TV works. Daddy had phoned Mommy and he had said, "Karen was right all along. We put Crystal Light in the tank again and she began swimming! She joined all the other fish."

All what other fish? I wondered.

That was when I realized that I had been dreaming. Crystal Light was still dead. I began to cry again.

I looked at my clock. It read 12:04. At least, I think it did. It was hard to tell. My tears made the numbers all blurry.

When I woke up the next morning, I felt awful. My eyes were scratchy, like sand was in them. And I was tired. I had woken up about six times between 12:04 and morning.

Oh, well. I knew I had to go to school. So I took off the clothes I had slept in. Then I looked in my closet. I pulled out the black velvet dress that is for special occasions. I put it on. Then I pulled on black tights and buckled on my black Mary Jane shoes. I tied a black ribbon in my hair.

Black is what people sometimes wear when they are sad that someone has died. (That is called being in mourning.)

Well, I was *very* sad about Crystal Light.

At breakfast, Seth said, "Good morning, Karen. Toast or cereal?"

"Neither," I said. I slumped into my seat. "I cannot eat a thing."

"Nothing?" asked Seth.

"Well, maybe some orange juice. I am in mourning."

Mrs. Dawes drove Nancy and me to school. Usually I talk a lot when we ride in the car. But that day I did not say anything. When we reached Stoneybrook Academy, Mrs. Dawes said, "Is something wrong, Karen?"

"My fish is dead," I told her. "My brother killed her. I am in mourning."

"Andrew killed Crystal Light?" shrieked Nancy.

"No. David Michael did. I'm not sure how, but he did it. Crystal Light died sometime yesterday."

"I'm sorry to hear that," said Mrs. Dawes as Nancy and I got out of the car. "I hope you feel better soon."

"Thank you," I answered in a small, sad voice.

Nancy started to run into school. I walked behind her very slowly.

"Come on, Karen!" called Nancy.

"I can't run," I told her. "I'm in mourning."

Finally we reached our classroom. (Nancy walked slowly with me.) The first person we saw was Hannie Papadakis.

"Karen!" exclaimed Hannie. "Why are you dressed like that?"

"Because David Michael killed Crystal Light yesterday. I'm in mourning."

"Oooh," said Hannie. "I'm sorry. . . . Karen, are you crying?"

I shook my head, even though I was starting to cry a little.

Hannie looked very concerned. "It'll be all right," she told me.

By the time Ms. Colman came into our room, practically everyone knew about Crystal Light. They felt very, very sorry for me. Even Pamela and Jannie and Leslie, who are my enemies.

"Your brother killed your fish?" cried Pamela. "That is just awful. How could anyone kill a helpless little fish? I'm sorry, Karen."

A Funeral for
Crystal Light

All that day I sat silently in my black
clothes. I did not eat lunch. At recess, I sat
on a rock and watched my friends play
games.

The next day, I decided that I was still in
mourning. So I put on the same black dress,
the same black tights, and the same black
shoes. I made one change, though. I did
not put the black ribbon in my hair. Instead,
I put on an old hat of Mommy's. I found it
in our dress-up box. It was black velvet

(which was good because it matched my dress). *And* it had a veil. I wore the hat with the veil covering my forehead and my eyes.

When I got to school that day, only Hannie and Nancy and Ricky (my husband) asked how I was feeling. Nobody else paid any attention. Except for Pamela. She said, "Nice hat, Karen." Then she and Jannie and Leslie began to giggle. I guess they were through feeling sorry for me.

Even my best friends seemed to have forgotten about me by recess. They did not notice when I sank down on the rock again. They did not ask me to play hopscotch or dodgeball. So I just sat with my head on my hands.

I am a very good moper.

Especially when I am in mourning.

It was while I was sitting on the rock, moping and mourning, that I got my idea. See, I was remembering another pet that had died. It was David Michael's collie, Louie. (David Michael got Shannon after

Louie died.) Anyway, David Michael was very upset after Louie died. So we held a funeral for Louie. We held it in our backyard. We played a song and everyone in my big-house family said something nice about Louie. We even made a cross for him. Then we buried his food dishes and his leash.

David Michael felt better after the funeral. (I guess we all did.) So now I wondered, Would a funeral for Crystal Light make me feel better?

Yes, I decided. At least planning it would make me feel better. I could stop thinking about my brother the fish-killer. Instead, I could think about the funeral.

Let's see. We would hold the funeral in the backyard at the big house. We would hold it tomorrow, Saturday, when Andrew and I were staying at Daddy's. We could have music and maybe we could sing a song. Then we would bury Crystal Light in her little white coffin.

By the end of school that day, I had decided that the funeral would begin at two o'clock. I invited all of my classmates to it, even Pamela and her friends. A lot of kids said they would come. Already I felt better.

The Fight

It was another Friday night at Daddy's house. I kept thinking about the last one. At the last Friday dinner, Andrew and I did not have a big-house pet yet. We had not even asked if we could get one. Now it was just two weeks later. Andrew had a pet. But my pet had already lived and died. (Fish-killer.) So I was still dressed in black, including the hat with the veil.

During dinner, I told my family about Crystal Light's funeral. "I know I should have asked permission before I invited

54

everyone over," I said. "But I was in a hurry. The funeral will be tomorrow. I wanted to make sure my friends could come. I hope that's all right."

"It's all right with *me*," said David Michael crossly. (He was still mad that I had called him a fish-killer.) "That little white box is getting smelly. I can hardly go into the playroom anymore. . . . But I do go in to take care of Goldfishie," he added hastily. He looked at Andrew. Then he went on, "We have to keep the door to the playroom closed. Otherwise this whole house would be stinky."

I almost said something really mean to David Michael. After all, it was his fault the playroom was stinky. Instead, I just narrowed my eyes at him. I gave him a mean-snake look.

Then I glanced around at the rest of my family. "At the funeral," I went on, "I think we should have music. So I will ask Natalie Springer to bring her violin. I will make the other funeral plans tonight. Oh, by the way, you are all invited to the funeral . . . except for David Michael."

"What?!" exclaimed David Michael. "How come I'm not invited?"

"Because you are a fish-killer. You killed Crystal Light."

"Karen," said Daddy warningly.

"Well, he did!" I cried.

"Did not," said David Michael.

"Did so, too."

"Did not so, too."

"Did too, did too!"

"Did not, did not!"

"All *right!*" said Daddy in a loud voice. His voice was so loud that he scared both Emily Michelle and Boo-Boo. Emily began to cry. Boo-Boo jumped a mile. Then he ran out of the kitchen. He skittered once on the slippery floor.

"Karen," Daddy went on. "You know very well that David Michael took good care of your fish."

"Oh, yeah? Then why is Crystal Light dead?" I asked.

"And smelly," muttered David Michael.

"I don't know," replied Daddy. "But Goldfishie is still alive and healthy. David Michael must be doing something right."

"Well, he did one thing wrong."

Kristy spoke up then. "Karen, I don't think you're being fair. I live here — "

"So do I," I interrupted.

"I know, but I mean I live here all the time," said Kristy patiently. "And I saw how carefully David Michael took care of the fish."

"Oh, you're just saying that because David Michael is your *real* brother."

"Karen," said Elizabeth, "in this house, you kids are all 'real' brothers and sisters, whether you have the same parents or not, or whether you're adopted."

"I don't care," I replied. "David Michael is a fish-killer, fish-killer, fish-killer."

Daddy stood up suddenly. (Uh-oh. That was a bad sign.) "Karen, go to your room this moment," he said. "You may stay there for half an hour."

Who Did Swallow Jonah?

I huffed upstairs to my room. With every step, I whispered, "Fish-killer, fish-killer, fish-killer." But I did not really mind my punishment.

I needed some quiet time in my room to plan Crystal Light's funeral. So as soon as I got there, I slammed the door shut. (I hoped Daddy heard that downstairs.) Then I sat at my table. I picked up a pencil. I began writing on a pad of paper.

Music. I had to have music for Crystal Light. As soon as my punishment was over,

I would call Natalie Springer and tell her to bring her violin to the funeral. Who cares if the only song she can play is "Twinkle, Twinkle, Little Star"? Not me.

After *Music* I wrote down *Speech*. Somebody should make a gigundo nice speech about Crystal Light. Isn't that what people usually do at funerals? Someone makes a speech and says how the person who died was honest and helpful and liked children and stuff. *I* should really be the one to make Crystal Light's speech. But I did not think I could do it without crying. I did *not* want to cry in front of the kids in my class. Especially Pamela, Leslie, and Jannie. When I was allowed to leave the room, I would ask Kristy if she would make a speech about Crystal Light.

Okay. *Music* and *Speech* were taken care of. Next I wrote down *Song*. I thought it would be nice if everyone sang a song for Crystal Light. It should be a song about a fish, of course. For the longest time, I just sat at my table and thought. There must not be very many songs about fish. Finally I remembered part of a song that Daddy used to sing to Andrew and me. It went: *Out in a meadow in a tiny-bitty pool fam fee itty fitties and their mama fitty, too. "Fim!" said the mama fitty . . .*

I trailed off. That did not sound quite right. Besides, it was much too silly a song for a sad, sad funeral.

I thought some more. The only other fish song I could come up with was one about Jonah and the whale. Our class had learned it in music that year. The first part of the song asks a question: *Who did, who did, who did, who did, who did swallow Jonah UP?* (The song is really much longer than that.) The second part of the song answers the question: *Whale did, whale did, whale did, whale did, whale did swallow Jonah DOWN!*

That song was sort of silly, too, but not nearly as silly as the one about the itty fitties. I decided it would be okay for Crystal Light's funeral. Besides, everyone in my class would know it.

The next thing I wrote on my pad of paper was *Burial*. I wanted to bury Crystal Light in her box next to Louie's cross. Her box would have to be very pretty. Tomorrow I would decorate it. I wished I could decorate it right now, but the box and Crystal Light were in the playroom.

Also, I would need someone to dig a hole to bury the box in. Maybe Sam or Charlie could do that. And, of course, I would need a tombstone. I would have to find one tomorrow. I would look for a nice flat rock. Then I would clean it up. Then I would write something on it. But what?

Maybe CRYSTAL LIGHT, R.I.P.

Or CRYSTAL LIGHT, ONLY ABOUT TWO WEEKS OLD.

Or CRYSTAL LIGHT — HER LIFE WAS SNUFFED OUT BY A FISH-KILLER.

That last one sounded dramatic. I liked it. I would decide tomorrow, though. Right now, my half an hour was almost up. I had lots of phone calls to make. It would be a busy evening.

Violins and Flowers

"Karen!" I heard Daddy call.

"Yes?"

"You may come out of your room now."

"Thank you," I replied.

Daddy was standing at the bottom of the stairs. I leaned over the railing in the hall outside my room. "May I make some private phone calls?" I asked Daddy. "May I use the phone in your room?"

"Yes," Daddy replied. (My punishment was over, but Daddy did not sound very happy with me. Maybe that was because I had not apologized to David Michael.)

Well, I was not going to apologize to a fish-killer. So I just said, "Thanks."

I walked down the hall to Daddy and Elizabeth's bedroom. I went inside and closed the door behind me. Then I flung myself across the bed. (That is a good position for talking on the phone.)

I called Natalie. "Can you play 'Twinkle, Twinkle, Little Star' at Crystal Light's funeral tomorrow?"

"Oh! Yes!" exclaimed Natalie. I could tell that she was happy I had asked her to play. In fact, Natalie was so happy that she began to cry. When she cries, she snorts. (This is a problem with Natalie. She cried and snorted when Ricky Torres and I got married. Oh, well. That is just the way Natalie is.)

Before we got off the phone, I said, "Oh, and bring a flower with you. And wear black, Natalie."

Then I called some of the kids in the big-house neighborhood. I invited them to the funeral. I told each one, "Bring a flower and wear black." The funeral was going to be very sad and somber.

I was just finishing up a call when I realized something. I had invited the kids in my class to Crystal Light's funeral. But I had not told them to wear black or to bring a flower.

So I made a list of all the kids in my class. I split it into three smaller lists. I called Nancy and asked her if she would mind calling the kids on one list. I called Hannie and asked her to call the kids on the second list. (I would take care of the third list myself.) I said to both Hannie and Nancy, "Tell everyone to wear black and to bring a flower. The flower can be paper if they can't find a real one."

Finally all of my calls had been made. I was gigundo tired. But I went to bed feeling good. Tomorrow, Crystal Light would have a very, very nice funeral.

"NO!"

The next morning, I jumped out of bed. Boy, did I have a lot to do that day. First, I found Kristy. She was in her bedroom. She was still in her pajamas.

" 'Morning," she said when she saw me. (She did not sound mad. I hoped that she had forgiven me for the fish-killer fight.)

" 'Morning," I replied. "Kristy? I have to ask you something important. Will you make a speech at Crystal Light's funeral this afternoon?"

"A speech?" repeated Kristy.

"Yes. One about what a terrific fish Crystal Light was. I don't want to do it because I'm afraid I will start to cry. And I don't want to cry in front of all my friends."

"Shall I say . . . ? Hmm. I don't know. But I will think of something," Kristy told me. "I'll think of nice things about Crystal Light."

Just hearing that made me cry. I could tell that the day was going to be very difficult. But I could handle it.

"Thank you," I said to Kristy. Then I left her room, sniffling.

The next thing I had to do was decorate Crystal Light's coffin. As more tears rolled down my cheeks, I thought about how yesterday I had decided that the coffin should look pretty. Now I was thinking that black is the color for funerals. Should I decorate Crystal Light's coffin with black designs?

No. Crystal Light was so shiny and pretty herself that she would want a colorful coffin. I was pretty sure of that.

I sat at my table with the coffin and a box of crayons. I thought for a long time. Finally I colored a rainbow on the lid of the box. It looked so beautiful that I began to cry again.

But I couldn't stop to cry for long. Now it was time to make a headstone for my poor, dead fish. I ran into our backyard. Then I slowed down. I walked around the yard. I looked carefully for a flat rock. I found lots of pebbles and stones. But a flat rock was harder to find. When I did find one, it was half buried in dirt and old leaves. So I took it inside and washed it in the kitchen sink.

I waited for it to dry. Then I put these words on it, in white paint:

CRYSTAL LIGHT, MY DELIGHT.
A LOVELY FISH.

The headstone was perfect, so I cried some more.

But I *still* had lots of work to do. I showed the headstone to Charlie. "Would you dig

a grave for Crystal Light?" I asked him. "I want her to be buried next to Louie's cross. Here is her headstone."

"Okay," said Charlie.

"Thank you," I replied. "Now remember. The funeral is at two o'clock. Everyone will be wearing black. And you should bring a flower."

"Okay," Charlie said again.

Then I had to find everybody else at the big house and tell *them* to wear black and bring flowers.

When I got to Elizabeth, I said, "And can you dress Emily in black and give her a flower to carry?"

Elizabeth said she would.

Okay. I had told everyone about the flowers and what to wear. Everyone except David Michael. But he knew what I was doing.

"Karen?" he said to me at lunchtime. "Can I *please* come to the funeral?"

"NO!" I cried.

David Michael looked hurt. At first, I thought he might tattle. But then I knew that he wouldn't. This was a problem between David Michael and me. We did not want any of the grown-ups to be part of it.

Crystal Light's Funeral.

It was a quarter to two. Everything and everybody was ready for the funeral. I was pleased. The big-house people were all in black, just like they had promised. Even Emily. And even David Michael. (I hoped he was not going to crash the funeral.) I was wearing my mourning outfit, including the hat and veil. I did not need to pretend to look sad, since I had cried all morning.

My family and I went outdoors. (David Michael was nowhere in sight.) A few moments later, Hannie and her brother, Linny, came over. Then Amanda and Max Delaney. By two o'clock, all of the neighborhood kids had arrived. About half of my class had arrived, too. I was relieved. Pamela, Leslie, and Jannie had not come.

I waited until five minutes after two. Then I stood in front of the crowd of people. I was holding Crystal Light in her coffin.

"Thank you for coming," I said to everyone. "And thank you for wearing black and bringing flowers." (Only a few kids had forgotten flowers.) "Crystal Light would have loved this," I went on. Then I said, "Okay, the funeral's beginning now. First, we will have some music by Natalie Springer."

Natalie was standing at the edge of the crowd. Her violin was in her hands. She stepped up beside me.

Screetch, screetch, scratch, scratch, went the violin. About halfway through the song I heard another sound: *Screetch, screetch, snort, snort.*

Natalie was crying. Oh, well.

As soon as the song was over, I thanked Natalie. I sent her back to the crowd. Then I called Kristy up front.

"And now," I said, "my sister Kristy has a speech about Crystal Light."

"Thank you," said Kristy. She was standing beside the tiny grave that Charlie had dug. "Today," she began, looking gigundo serious, "we mourn the loss of Crystal Light, a very special goldfish. For those of you who did not know her, Crystal Light was an excellent swimmer. She was graceful in the water. And she was pretty. It is no wonder that Karen called her 'Crystal Light, my delight.' "

I thought I would start crying when Kristy said that, but I did not. Ricky was looking at me. So were some other kids. I held in my tears. But I did not hear the rest of Kristy's speech.

When Kristy was finished, I asked everyone to sing "Who Did Swallow Jonah?" Only the kids in my class knew the song, though. They were sort of embarrassed to sing it by themselves. So the song sounded weak.

I tried to sing loudly to make up for this. *"WHALE DID SWALLOW JONAH DOWN!"* I yelled out the last line of the song.

"And *now*," I said, when everyone was quiet, "it is time to bury my dear little goldfish, Crystal Light."

I stepped over to the grave. Very gently, I set the white box in it. I looked at the rainbow one last time. Then I buried the box with the dirt Charlie had dug up. (It was in a pile next to the grave.)

"I hope you will be happy here," I whispered. "Or in fish heaven. Or wherever you go."

And then I did start to cry. But it was all right. My friends could not see me. My back was to them. I sort of had to take my time with the burying, though. I had to wait until my tears had dried. I could not brush them away because my hands were too dirty.

At last I was finished.

"Charlie?" I said.

Charlie stepped forward. He knew what to do. He drove the headstone into the ground. Now Crystal Light's headstone was next to Louie's cross.

And Crystal Light was really gone.

The End

Crystal Light was gone, but the funeral was not over. I wanted my fish's grave to look as pretty as the coffin. As pretty as Crystal Light. That morning, I had taken some of the gravel out of Goldfishie's aquarium. The gravel was bright blue. I had put it in a plastic bag and hidden the bag in the bushes.

Now I found the bag and opened it up. I poured the gravel over Crystal Light's grave. It looked like the bottom of the ocean. Perfect.

I turned to the people who had been watching me. "Thank you all for coming," I said. "The funeral is over now. As you leave, would you please put your flowers on top of the gravel? Thank you again."

Somehow, everyone formed a line. They filed past Crystal Light's grave, dropping their flowers on it. Most of the flowers were paper, but that was okay. They were very colorful.

My big-house family went inside.

The kids left — except for Hannie and Nancy. I wanted the Three Musketeers to be together. I needed my best friends.

We stood looking at the grave. It was covered with a huge mound of flowers. For awhile, we just stared at them. Then I said, "I guess it's over. The end. Crystal Light would have wanted it this way."

"I think so, too," said Nancy.

"So do I," said Hannie.

"It really is beautiful," I added.

"Yup," said Nancy.

"Yup," said Hannie.

We were not sure what to say to each other. Or, at least, Hannie and Nancy were not sure what to say to me. That was okay. I understood. Sometimes it is hard to know what to say to someone when that person is feeling sad.

After a long time, Nancy spoke up. "Karen, you didn't cry at the funeral today."

"Yes, I did. You just didn't see me," I replied.

"Oh," said Nancy. "Well, that is good. You should be able to cry, especially with your friends. When my grandfather died, our family sat *shiva* for a week." (Nancy and her family are Jewish.)

"What's *shiva*?" asked Hannie.

"It's a time when your relatives and friends come over. Daddy said it was a time when we could grieve for Papa. You know, feel bad about him. And our friends helped us. Just by being there."

I was thinking about what Nancy was saying when a voice called to us from somewhere.

"Hey, Karen! Hey, you guys!"

It was David Michael's voice. But I could not see him anywhere.

"That's David Michael," I whispered to Hannie and Nancy.

"Where is he?" asked Hannie. "And why are you whispering?"

"I'm not sure where he is. And I'm whispering because David Michael is probably up to something. I wouldn't let him come to the funeral."

"Because he's a fish-killer?" Nancy wanted to know.

Before I could answer, David Michael called again. "You *guys!* Come *here!*"

"I think he's in Morbidda Destiny's yard," said Hannie shakily.

"What do you want?" I yelled back.

"Just come here! I have to show you something!"

I looked at my friends uncertainly. Then I said, "We might as well go. But watch out for a trap. David Michael is mad at me."

The Hidden Pond

Nancy and Hannie and I walked slowly to the edge of my yard. We looked into Morbidda Destiny's yard. We could not see David Michael.

"Maybe it's not David Michael calling to us," whispered Hannie. "Maybe it's the witch herself. You know, they can disguise their voices and stuff."

I almost said, "That's silly, Hannie." But I changed my mind. Hannie was right. Maybe it *was* the witch. After all, David

Michael was mad at me. Why would he want to show me some —

"Wait a second," I said to the two other Musketeers. "If David Michael wants to show us something, it must be gross. Why would he be nice to me?"

"Then it *is* the witch!" shrieked Hannie.

"SHH! No it isn't," I told her. "I think it's David Michael tricking us." Then I raised my voice. "David Michael!" I called. "How can we see the something if we don't know where you are?"

"Oh. Sorry," replied David Michael. He stepped out from behind a bush. "Here I am," he said.

"Well, what are you doing?" I asked. "You're on the witch's property."

"I didn't want to miss the funeral," David Michael replied. "I knew I wasn't supposed to come, so I hid here and watched. When the funeral was over, I was on my way home. That's when I found this."

"Found what?"

"You'll have to come see for yourselves."

"Are you sure it's safe?" I wanted to know.

"No sign of Morbidda Destiny," replied David Michael.

I looked at Hannie and Nancy. We shrugged. Then Nancy said, "We might as well go."

I nodded. "Okay. Here we come," I called to my brother.

My friends and I tiptoed across the lawn to David Michael. I'm not sure what we were afraid of. But I kept expecting something to happen.

Nothing did. Not until we reached David Michael. Then he just pointed into some bushes. At first, all Hannie and Nancy and I could see was green. Green bushes, green stuff trailing across the ground. A green garden. But when we looked more closely, we saw something flashing in the sunlight.

"Water . . ." I said.

"Not just water. A fish pond," David

Michael told me. "It's okay to go closer. There's sort of a path to it."

David Michael led Hannie and Nancy and me toward the hidden pool.

"Ooh. It's beautiful," I said.

Around the little pond was a ring of rocks. And *in* the pond were . . . goldfish! Lots of them.

David Michael and my friends and I stood at the edge of the water.

"Wow. I don't believe it!" exclaimed Hannie.

"Look at *that* fish," said Nancy, pointing. "I think it's the prettiest."

"And *that* one must be the biggest," said Hannie, pointing, too.

"Yeah, it's twice the size of Goldfishie," agreed David Michael.

"Look over there. Look at that fish," said Nancy.

But I did not have a chance to. I felt an elbow nudging my ribs. I turned around to tell Hannie to quit it. But she was staring

at something behind me. Her eyes were very wide — and scared.

I turned to my other side. On the rocks next to me was a pair of pointy black shoes. And a pair of legs wearing black stockings . . .

Witch Fish

I looked up and up. I saw a long black dress. Over the dress was a black cape. And above that was Morbidda Destiny's face.

The witch.

I was so surprised that I stumbled. I would have fallen into the fish pond if Hannie hadn't grabbed me.

For a moment, no one spoke.

Then suddenly David Michael exploded. "I wasn't doing anything bad! Honest!" he exclaimed. "See, my sister's goldfish died. She wouldn't let me come to the funeral.

But I really wanted to see it anyway. So I hid over here and watched. And when I was coming home, I saw the little path and I followed it. It led to this pond. I thought Karen would want to see the fish. So I called her and her friends over. They walked on the path, too. We didn't step on any of your plants. We're just looking at the fish."

"They're very pretty," added Nancy.

"So you lost your fish?" Morbidda Destiny asked me. (I nodded.) "How did it die?" she wanted to know. (I shrugged.) "Well, fish are tricky pets."

David Michael gave me a Look. Then he turned to Morbidda Destiny. "I'm sorry if we hurt anything. Or if we scared you," he said.

(*We* scared the *witch?*)

"Well, *I'm* sorry to hear about the fish," said Morbidda Destiny.

"Her name was Crystal Light," I said sadly.

The witch nodded. Then she turned to leave. (Her cape swirled around.) "You children stay here. I'll be right back," she said.

As soon as the witch was out of sight, Hannie said, "Okay, she's gone. Now's our chance to escape."

"Yeah," agreed Nancy. "Let's go. Before Morbidda Destiny puts a spell on us. How do we know where these fish came from? Maybe they're all people the witch turned into fish. And we would be three more witch fish for her pond."

"Ooh." Hannie shivered.

But I glanced at David Michael. He was looking at me and smiling.

"*I'm* staying here," I said. "Morbidda Destiny sounded very sorry about Crystal Light. She must like fish a lot. Maybe she knows a spell that will bring Crystal Light back to life. Maybe she had to get some special herbs — "

Before I could finish, the witch was running through her yard toward us.

"Darn!" exclaimed Hannie. "We missed our chance."

Morbidda Destiny was clutching something small. It was a fishnet.

"Yikes!" squealed Nancy. "I was right!"

But the witch handed the net to *me*. She
said, "Choose a fish. Catch it in the net.
Take it home. Then you will have another
fish."

"Really? Thank you!" I said. I took the
fishnet from the witch. I gazed into the
pond. I was looking for a fish like Crystal
Light. And suddenly I found one. She was
Crystal Light's size, and she had a black
spot on her tail. I scooped her up before I
lost sight of her.

I held up the net. Inside it, the new
goldfish wriggled. The sunlight caught the
shiny scales. It made them look more golden
than ever.

"Thank you," I said to Morbidda Destiny
again. Then I added, "I better get this new
fish into the tank right away. Come on, you
guys."

David Michael, Nancy, and Hannie followed me down the path.

"I'll bring your net back as soon as I can!" I called to the witch.

Then I raced toward the big house. I could not believe how lucky I was. Or how nice the witch had been.

Crystal Light
the Second

Karen, Hannie, David Michael, and I ran to the playroom in the big house. "Hey, Andrew!" I called as we tore past his room.

"What?" he yelled back.

"Come to the playroom. I have something to show you."

Andrew arrived just in time to see me lower my new fish into the tank. "Aughh!" he screamed. "Crystal Light came back to life! I thought that couldn't happen."

"It didn't, silly. This is a new fish. Morbidda Destiny gave her to me."

"You put a witch fish in the same tank as Goldfishie?" cried Andrew.

"I don't think she's a witch fish." I told Andrew the story of what had happened in Morbidda Destiny's backyard.

When I finished, Andrew still looked worried. But Nancy saved the day. She changed the subject by saying, "Why don't you name your new fish, Karen? She needs a name."

"Hmm. You're right," I replied. "Let's see."

"How about Whoopy?" suggested Hannie.

"For a beautiful fish? No way!" I answered.

"How about Fred?" said David Michael.

"That's a boy's name."

"Okay, then Freddie."

I shook my head. I was thinking, Miranda? Goldie? Esther? (Esther Williams was this old-timey star that Daddy and Elizabeth like to watch in black-and-white movies. She was a very excellent swimmer.)

"You know what?" I said at last. "I chose this fish because she looks so much like Crystal Light. So I am going to name her Crystal Light the Second."

We watched Goldfishie and Crystal Light the Second swim in their tank. They seemed to be getting along. We watched them until Nancy's father came to pick her up, and Hannie said she had to go home, too. When David Michael and I were alone in the playroom I said, "I'm *really* sorry about our fight."

"That's okay," replied David Michael.

"I'm sorry I wouldn't let you come to the funeral. And I'm especially sorry that I called you a fish-killer. You know what? I didn't really think you killed Crystal Light. But I was mad that she was dead. And I had to yell at someone, so I yelled at you. That was not very nice."

"No," agreed David Michael. "It wasn't. But that's okay, too."

"So you forgive me?"

"Yes."

"What are you smiling about?" I asked.

"You still have to return Morbidda Destiny's fishnet. You have to go back to the witch's house. . . . And I'm not going with you."

I made a face. But then I picked up the net and headed downstairs. I walked through our back door. The first thing I saw were the two graves. Still holding the net, I sat beside Crystal Light's grave. I touched the pil of f███████'s.

Then I said, I did not really have a chance to say good-bye to you today, Crystal Light. So I will say it now. Good-bye, Crystal Light, my delight. I hope there's a fish heaven somewhere, and that it is very, very beautiful, and that you are swimming around in it.

"I hope you don't mind that I got another fish and named her after you. I am not replacing you with her. I just got her because I miss you so much.

"Well, that's all I can think of. For now. But maybe I will talk to you some other times."

I stood up. Then I headed bravely toward Morbidda Destiny's house.

About the Author

ANN M. MARTIN lives in New York City and loves ani█████████er cat, Mouse, knows how to take the p█████ off the hook.

Other books by Ann M. Martin that you might enjoy are *Stage Fright*, *Me and Katie (the Pest)*, and the books in *The Baby-sitters Club* series.

Ann likes ice cream, the beach, and *I Love Lucy*. And she has her own little sister, whose name is Jane.

Little Sister

Don't miss #17

KAREN'S BROTHERS

All that day I would talk only to Elizabeth, Nannie, Kristy, Emily Michelle, and Shannon. At first my brothers and Daddy kept saying, "What's wrong?"

I did not answer them.

Then, at dinnertime, Dav▓▓▓chael said, "I think Karen is mad at▓▓."

"At who?" asked Andrew.

"Us boys."

"Me, too?" said Daddy. "I haven't done anything."

I leaned over to Kristy. I whispered, "I'm not speaking to *any* boys. They are all jerks. Tell them I said that."